Gwendles Powell was born to English parents but was brought up in Rome, Italy. She moved to London, England when she was twelve years old and continued her education to then go to Drama School. She has been an actress and producer for many years and has won many awards but has now turned her hand to writing.

Dedicated to my daughter Isabella, one day you will understand.

Wendy Powell, my mother & always my inspiration.

In Memoriam
My father, Peter John Powell.

Gwendles Powell

CHILDREN ARE NOT PERMITTED TO PLAY ON THIS LAWN

AUSTIN MACAULEY PUBLISHERS™

LONDON • CAMBRIDGE • NEW YORK • SHARJAH

A CIP catalogue record for this title is available from the British Library.

ISBN 9781398425378 (Paperback)
ISBN 9781398425385 (ePub e-book)

www.austinmacauley.com

First Published 2022
Austin Macauley Publishers Ltd®
1 Canada Square
Canary Wharf
London
E14 5AA

I would like to thank Alex French for his collaboration & contribution.

I would like to thank Jem, one of my oldest friends for his support, assistance & contribution to the book & its journey.

I would like to thank the following people who have helped me immeasurably; Jane Lancaster, and Neil Lancaster.

Thank you to Liz Francis for her continuous support.

To Carolyn Bayley, for all her encouragement and to the rest of the Bayley Family, Michael, Steuart & Hugo for all their support they have given me throughout this journey and I thank them so much.

A big thank you to Jim Coughlan.

Book One
Nine and Three Quarters

Chapter 1

I was always up to mischief running around making noise. I was usually in quiet places where children were not allowed to play. I would be so interested in wildlife and nature and usually pick daisies, which I would give to my mum, and place them in the palm of her hand.

However, when my parents were not looking, I would collect bugs and insects with my best friend, Tom. He would always find the beetles and centipedes and would squeal with delight when he found a dandelion. Together, we would sit down on the grass and blow the puffballs that would disperse into the wind.

It made me giggle when I showed my parents what I had collected. My mum would inevitably scream, my dad would try not to laugh, as out of my pocket would appear a spider and a slug!

Chapter 2

Great Granny's tea parties were full of fun.

I called her Gragra, as Great Granny was too much of a mouthful to say.

I would always run to her kitchen and open all her biscuit tins, which were full of chocolate and small scrumptious cakes.

The experience was far too overwhelming that I would jump up and down and squeal with delight. Great Granny would laugh, holding onto her chair as my exuberance made her feel quite dizzy!

My love for sweets made it a mere impossibility for me to sit quietly.

It was impossible.

Well, what can you expect if you are only three!

Chapter 3

We were four generations of women.

On several occasions, Granny, whom I called Grandma, would organise our photo-shoot and get my granddad to be the photographer.

He would reluctantly take the photos, as he found it difficult to get us all to smile at the same time.

He would aim the camera at us all. Inevitably, it would all go wrong. Gragra would always speak or shut her eyes. I would look bored and cross as I hated what I was wearing and Grandma would look frustrated as the photo-shoot wasn't going to plan.

My mother would find the whole situation so amusing that she would try to contain her fit of giggles by pretending to sneeze.

Chapter 4

Dad couldn't be there as he was always working far away. I think it was far away.

However, when he returned, he would make me laugh and giggle and would give me one penny.

He would always say that I should keep my pennies as one day, they would be very important. He would state,

"Remember, Noelle, always keep your pennies."

I hated the name Noelle as my friends nicknamed me Christmas, which I found slightly awkward but in the end I grew to like it and felt rather special.

Chapter 5

My mum tried to work but found it difficult as I kept on coming home from nursery with lice and then chicken pox.

Unfortunately, I gave my mum the chicken pox, which resulted in us both staying home with spots and rather itchy heads!

I was the only child and felt alone at times when most of my friends had brothers and sisters.

I so wanted to have a brother or a sister. I remember asking my mum, "Can you give me a brother, please, or a sister?

"How can I have one? Dad gives me pennies when he comes home. I've saved them, so we can buy a brother or a sister at the shop? Please, Mummy!"

Chapter 6

My mum looked at me in an endearing way. I will always remember her look full of chicken pox and one spot was right at the end of her nose!

"Noelle," she explained. "I can't buy a baby at the shop. Mum and Dad have to make one."

"How?" I retorted.

"Does the baby come to you like magic?"

"Yes, Noelle, children are magic," she had said.

Such enchanting words.

But her spot at the end of her nose was most distracting.

It made me giggle, it still does to this day.

Chapter 7

Shortly afterwards I was taken out of nursery as I was due to start my first day of school.

I was so nervous. It was daunting. I really hoped I wouldn't be nicknamed Christmas. However, my dad explained, "You are so well loved by us. You can say why you are called Noelle as you were born on Christmas day."

The first day of school was nerve-racking. I felt grown up and to my delight, my music teacher was also called Noelle!

I returned from school and was so happy and excited. I loved my school and felt at home.

My dad had to return to work which made me sad as he worked far away.

He would suppress his tears whilst saying, "I have to go but will count the days until I return."

With those words, he gave me a hug and then kissed my mum and waved goodbye.

Chapter 8

That evening something extraordinary happened.

I ran to my mum with complete excitement. I could barely talk. "Mum, Mummy…I've seen a thing…in the sky, a thing, a Frisbee, a circle with lights!"

She was cooking and spoke, in rather a distracted way, "Noelle, it must be a plane."

I began to jump up and down as I couldn't explain in words the magnitude of the situation. It was far too overwhelming.

I began to speak, trying to breathe, "No. No…Mummy…Mum. It's…it's…I don't know. A flying round thing, a disc, oh, I don't know…come and see it. It's in the sky…above the garden!"

She followed me into the garden and to her astonishment, she saw what I saw. With a sense of calm and serenity, she uttered, "Noelle, this is a special moment; a moment that you and I will remember for the rest of our lives."

With those words we saw the flying frisbee ascend into the sky.

Chapter 9

I went to sleep that night, excited and overwhelmed. I had seen a gargantuan frisbee surrounded by intricate fairy lights. I had so many questions, so many thoughts and smiled whilst I drifted off to sleep…a deep, profound sleep, a sleep that led me to float.

I gently moved upwards towards the midnight sky, where the moon's reflection dazzled the shimmering stars.

I continued to drift higher and higher towards a lonely star, then with a jolt, I plummeted onto a chair surrounded by kids watching a beauty pageant show!

Chapter 10

I rubbed my eyes, extremely confused. I scanned my surroundings, examined the kids and noticed they wore similar clothing.

They wore jeans together with white or grey tops.

It seemed like a uniform of some kind but something bothered me but couldn't fathom out what it was.

I continued to observe when out of nowhere, a very loud and abrupt noise echoed throughout the whole auditorium.

It made me jump and quite honestly, it was so loud that I fell onto the lap of a girl sitting next to me!

I apologised profusely, but she didn't seem to hear as all her attention was firmly directed towards the stage.

Chapter 11

I turned towards the stage where a boy wearing a huge blue and silver cloak stood smiling and holding a microphone. He had such a wide grin that it made me smile to the fact that it seemed so contagious that the whole audience started to smile.

He took a deep breath and loudly announced with pride and delight, "The winner of this year's contest…is…" There was a pause but a pause that felt slightly too long.
He looked scared and uncomfortable. He desperately tried to speak but fear had made its ugly descent that his beautiful glowing face turned so pale that it looked as if he had forgotten to breathe.

The cold silence continued and then miraculously, the audience of kids started to clap slowly. Then they began to chant. "You can do it, Ralph. You can do it. Come on, Ralph. Don't be scared, you can do it!"

Chapter 12

Ralph took a deep breath, brought the microphone to his lips and with all his strength and might proclaimed, "And the winner is…" He then paused, took another breath and with great confidence announced, "And the winner is Peter!"

The kids in the audience started to clap and cheer whilst they shouted, "Well done, Ralph! Well done!"

Ralph smiled.

When all of a sudden, a tall blonde boy, rather elegant in stature, appeared at Ralph's side.

He took the microphone and projected over the excitable audience. "Ralph, you spoke on stage. You have overcome your fears. We are so proud of you and other things…which we are all aware of."

The clapping continued whilst Ralph waved to the audience. His moon like face glowed once more.

He seemed so happy.

Chapter 13

I thought what other things did Ralph get over.

I wanted to know. Ralph was so lovely.

I would have hugged him but it might have been inappropriate seeing I didn't know him.

Actually, I didn't know anyone and quite honestly didn't know where I was!

I continued to look at Peter on stage.

I thought he was really handsome. He looked like all the other kids wearing jeans and a white top.

Then without any warning he took his top off!

I stared motionless.

He was completely see-through!

Chapter 14

I just stared. Stunned at seeing his see-through lungs!

They were absolutely beautiful, they sparkled.

I watched his bright red heart pump the blood around his see-through body.

I couldn't believe what I was seeing!

His liver and kidneys were vibrant, in fact, all of his organs were dazzling with colour!

Peter continued to walk around the stage whilst everyone clapped and cheered.

Suddenly, a bright light illuminated throughout his body.

It was mesmerising, it was magical!

Chapter 15

A girl next to me whispered, "I knew Peter would win. He is the most beautiful out of all of us on this planet. His soul shines so bright."

"Yes," I replied, "but, excuse me, what planet?"

She retorted, "Our planet."

All of a sudden, a loud noise echoed throughout the auditorium. We all watched in silence as Peter began to speak.

Not only was Peter on stage but a shadow seemed to hover around him.

Peter smiled and uttered, "You all know we have a new friend amongst us." Everyone glanced towards to where I was sitting.

I froze, hoping it wasn't me, just wanted to wake up at home as everything started to look rather odd and feel rather odd.

Chapter 16

"Noelle, welcome to our world. Come up on stage and talk to us!"

My heart sank to my toe. I thought, *talk! Talk about what?* I was seeing a boy who was completely see through, albeit his face was like mine, nevertheless. I found it all incredulous and very hard to comprehend.

The kids started to clap but were more interested in trying to locate where I was sitting.

I froze to my chair and started to crouch so that none of the kids could spot me.

The girl sitting beside me uttered, "Noelle, we have been expecting you. My name is Daisy."

I smiled whilst I looked into her huge, dark eyes, contemplating my escape without anyone noticing.

Chapter 17

Daisy gripped my shoulder. "No, you can't leave Noelle!"

I thought that maybe she had read my mind.

I tried to keep my mind blank in order for her not to scrutinise my thoughts. Unfortunately, as hard as I tried to think of nothing, my thoughts kept on popping up. It was so hard not to think of my escape!

She smiled and giggled, which confirmed my suspicion that she had read my mind. I scanned her face and noticed that her black glowing skin and black satin hair seemed to sparkle.

I really had thought I was looking at an angel.

Chapter 18

Daisy continued to speak. "Peter has won because of his glowing soul. You must go up on stage and talk about your world. We have been expecting you for some time." I plucked up some form of courage and started to walk towards the stage, full of dread. My knees had become numb. I had absolutely no feeling in my hands as nerves encompassed my whole body.

I arrived to the stage where Peter gave me the microphone. "Hello," he whispered. "I know you are nervous, but we are so happy to finally meet you." I smiled awkwardly whilst I addressed the audience.

I managed to utter something like, "Um, not quite sure why I am here…um…err." Then I paused as I started to see an audience of kids staring at me in the most curious way.

Chapter 19

They all put on their glasses and to my amazement, they became see through. I was stunned I couldn't speak. I became hot and then cold. Peter then put his glowing see through arm around me and uttered, "Don't worry, we are your friends."

I looked at him and stuttered, "Why…um, why am I here?"

He continued, "We have been watching you for a long time, you are curious and bright but most of all, you have a beautiful soul."

I stared into Peter's eyes. They were piercing blue or maybe brown or black or even green as they kept on changing! I felt quite dizzy as I tried to focus on his multi-coloured eyes.

Chapter 20

I uttered a few words which really didn't make any sense whatsoever. He grinned in a see-through way that, quite honestly, my heart might have done a somersault. I wasn't sure as I then couldn't breathe as I found his beauty far too overwhelming.

In a gentle tone he uttered, "Noelle, do you like fishing?" I couldn't believe what I had just heard, thought the subject was quite bewildering.

I replied, "Excuse me? What? So sorry, um, yes, have been fishing. I think, yes, with my dad." Peter seemed distracted as his attention turned towards a bright light from somewhere up there, not sure where.

The light and its shadow started to descend. I watched motionless through the silence as the light unfolded the most beautiful sphinx like cat I had ever seen. She stoically made her descent to the stage, greeting the audience of kids by bowing to them in a form of complete respect.

I just watched, I don't think I took a breath as I was slightly terrified when the majestic beauty turned her attention to me.

Candidly, she approached me. Her penetrating deep blue eyes gazed into mine whilst she spoke in a rather stoic way.

"Noelle, I am so glad to meet you. You have met the children of our world. The adults don't live amongst us. Some live on earth and are saving us day by day."

Chapter 21

Then in an echoing voice full of trepidation and demise. She stood on her back legs and stated, "I am Zaphire, the keeper and protector of souls. I protect and help all I can." She then turned to the audience and continued, "But, look at my children!"

I turned towards the audience of kids and noticed that none of the see-through children were the same. They were missing parts of themselves.

I looked closer, some of them missing parts of their heart, some parts of their lungs, kidneys, limbs but they still glowed.

Their souls still glowed but they weren't all intact.

The cat then moved much closer to me. She had the most penetrating blue eyes, the most astonishing cat I had ever seen. She meandered around me whilst speaking. "Noelle, I want you to save my children, my children are helping your planet. They are helping as many children as they can but we need help. Their souls need energising so that they can give…"

All of a sudden Peter interrupted her, "Zaphire, I am so sorry to intrude but Noelle needs to go home. It's too much information for now."

Chapter 22

Zaphire bowed and turned to the kids in the audience, who then took off their glasses and miraculously became human again. She then beckoned to the girl that was previously sitting next to me. "Daisy, guide Noelle home."

I ran to Daisy. "Daisy, I am scared, what's happening? Some of you without hearts or lungs or arms or legs. Why?"

She replied, "Even though we are not complete, we try to enjoy what we have." With those words she guided me back to sleep.

Chapter 23

I drifted into a deep and profound sleep, glided past the moon and the stars, floated and started my descent back to earth.

Startled I woke up in my bed, ran to my mum who was sleeping. Exasperated and excited, I exclaimed, "Mum, Mummy, I saw the see-through people. Wake up, Mummy. Wake up!" I started to shout, "Mummy, wake up!"

Mum never woke up.

Chapter 24

My whole world fell apart. My father rushed back from far away. My granny and grandpa distressed mourning their only child, nonetheless, trying to be brave for me.

Gragra was all in a tither, I couldn't stop crying.

My mum gone, it was inconceivable.

The funeral was refined, it was simple.

Just close friends and family in a circle around the coffin.

I placed a Daisy at its centre with a small note saying, "I will love you forever."

Chapter 25

Great Granny made a fuss exclaiming to the priest, "Will you speak up. I can't hear a word!"

My granny uttered quietly to Gragra, "You must put your earpiece in!"

Gragra retorted, "Nonsense child, the priest needs to articulate!"

My father held my hand and we looked at one another whilst he whispered, "It's you and me now, kiddo. We have to be strong. Mum would want you to still laugh and be the you, you have always been."

My friend, Tom, was also standing next to me. We usually would laugh all the time together but this time we both cried.

My granny continued to cry, held by Grandpa whilst Gragra started to get restless and with impatience proclaimed, "I have had enough!" And with those words, she confidently moved towards the priest, who was in mid sermon. Exasperated, she bellowed,

"You do realise that none of us can hear you…give me the microphone. I will speak!"

Chapter 26

We all turned round as Gragra got hold of the microphone. "I want to talk and what I will say is that my darling Granddaughter had a gift, an extraordinary gift. She was fun, had a sense of humour, loved her family, loved life and was extremely successful at whatever she set out to achieve. She was and is so loved by all of us. Her love will now protect little Noelle."

With that statement she gave back the microphone to the priest and whispered, "That is how you do it, you must project!"

The priest smiled and continued the SERVICE.

Chapter 27

Life became discombobulated. I ended up living with my grandparents whilst my dad still had to work far away, which saddened me so.

Granny and Grandpa gave me cuddles and tried to give me a normal life as much as deemed possible. However, my friend, Tom, was always a great help.

He would pop around and we would have dinner with Granny and Grandpa and notoriously, we would get the giggles over no particular reason.

It was so comforting to have such a lovely friend. Actually, he was the brother I never had.

My grandparents tried so desperately hard to help me with my homework. It made me smile whilst they got in a state, whilst having great discussions over my Math's and English papers! I often knew the answers to the questions but wanted them to be involved in my work, which gave them a sense of purpose and in a way great pride.

Grandpa would be so frustrated. "It's all so different. In my day it used to be so straightforward. Now it's just something else!"

Granny would overcompensate by baking cakes as it all got too much. She was a fantastic cook and her cakes were scrumptious. "David, please, the Math's is getting us all in a tither. It's different now a days." She would wink at me, knowing a lovely cake would calm Grandpa down whilst he tried so desperately hard to help me. In a way it was so endearing and it made me love him so.

Chapter 28

I was meticulous in nature, very organised and really enjoyed Mathematics and Sciences. I loved problem solving and in a way, it distracted me from missing my dad and, of course, the deep and horrible pain of the loss of my mum.

My dad would come home from work most weekends. Bringing me daisies and as always, my one penny. However, on one occasion, he brought me something quite special.

A bundle was in his arms covered by a blanket. My curiosity was far too overwhelming that I forgot to say hello, as was trying to control myself from jumping up and down with pure excitement.

He smiled. "I have a surprise for you, Noelle." The bundle started to move and then started to yelp. Dad removed the blanket and to my greatest joy appeared an adorable puppy.

I couldn't utter a word. I was so grateful and utterly speechless. Tears of joy ran down my father's cheeks whilst he gently placed the puppy in my arms. I just uttered the words, "Thank you." There weren't any other words that I could express. There wasn't another thing that I could say.

All I did know was that a veil of sadness and solitude had lifted giving us all a glimpse of hope once again.

Chapter 29

Days and months passed and life felt so much better.

Grandma and Grandpa were completely enamoured by puppy.

He changed our lives.

We laughed again.

We enjoyed going to the park much more. Long walks at weekends as with great joy, my grandfather loved planning routes.

The walks were rather long; both puppy and I felt exhausted when we got home and very hungry. Granny always had something yummy ready for us to eat, which we relished with great enthusiasm.

Life was happier with my new best friend in our lives and school became more interesting, especially with classes on sex education!

Chapter 30

My eyes would open wide when the teacher talked about sex and making babies.

We all started to giggle. Some of us uncontrollably when the teacher went into great detail by putting a big willy on her desk and explaining, "The penis goes into the vagina."

I don't think we heard much more as the whole class got into hysterics.

My good friend, Molly, and I were sent out of the classroom due to our uncontrollable laughter.

All parents were extremely angry that the sex education talk had taken place without prior warning as they wanted to tell us themselves that it wasn't the stalk that brought us to our parents.

Unbeknown to them, we knew the facts a long time ago!

Chapter 31

I remember telling Granny and Grandpa about the sex education talk. Great Granny had come over for tea.

I started talking about the lesson whilst Gragra had her sandwich in one hand and listened quite attentively and not realising that puppy took the sandwich out of her hand. Still holding an invisible sandwich, she exclaimed, "Are we talking about sex?"

"Please!" Granny retorted. "I was explaining to Noelle that when two people love each other…"

Gragra interrupted, "Oh, stop! What nonsense. I remember when…"

"Stop, please!" Granny proclaimed. Then started to have a coughing fit.

She usually did when she got nervous.

Gragra continued with great glee, "Well, I find this matter extremely entertaining."

I laughed at not only Gragra being able to hear most acutely over the word sex, but her eyesight also seemed to be on top form. She realised that puppy had been eating her sandwiches all along!

We had a lovely tea and puppy and I went to bed very contented in having a fun evening.

Chapter 32

I went to bed and started to drift off to sleep, into a deep sleep and started to float and ascended into the sky.

I got excited thinking I would see my friends from the other world. I drifted up and floated towards the lonely star and with a jolt found myself in a playground. I saw Daisy and ran towards her. "Daisy!" I proclaimed.

She hugged me. We were so happy to see each other.

She then announced, "Noelle, it's my birthday today, come here." I ran towards her proclaiming,

"I thought I would never see you again."

Daisy ignored what I said. "Look, Noelle, look at my presents!"

I couldn't see any presents; thought she might have imagined them. "Excuse me? Sorry, can't see any presents." She then laughed.

"No, the other me has the presents you can touch. I feel what the other me feels."

Perplexed, I continued to speak, "I don't understand, Daisy."

I thought she might have been rather confused, then stopped my thoughts as I remembered she could read my mind! She started to giggle as of course did I.

Chapter 33

Suddenly, we all stopped playing and remained very still.

I looked above where I saw Peter and Zaphire make their descent.

Peter decided to show himself as a human whilst Zaphire was in her usual translucent form.

Zaphire beckoned Ralph to join them.

She looked proud whilst he made his way towards her.

I whispered to Daisy, "What's happening? Why has Ralph been asked to join them?"

She replied, "His clone has been ill as you know. Remember he found it hard to speak at the pageant show?"

I retorted, "He was scared, that's all. It's not an illness!"

Chapter 34

Zaphire began to speak with a controlled and echoing voice. "We have managed to cure Ralph's clone. We never knew how to heal sadness, anxiety or fear. It is a human emotion that we cannot comprehend."

I just stared transfixed whilst she approached to where we were all standing. She continued to speak with humility in her voice, "With our extensive research, we have been able to help our earthlings overcome this emotion."

All of a sudden, she pranced towards the kids whilst nodding respectfully to each and every one of them.

Chapter 35

Bewildered by the situation, I watched her approach me. I started to get anxious, thinking she might pounce. I was terrified. I think I had forgotten to breathe but then to my relief, she stopped. I took a deep breath whilst we just looked at each other for a moment which seemed timeless. Her deep blue eyes gave me a sense of calm and serenity. I actually felt happy. An emotion I hadn't felt for a very long time. It was as if Zaphire had taken away the pain, suffering and sorrow that filtered throughout my being. I finally felt myself again. I was finally at peace.

I gazed with wonder into Zaphire's penetrating eyes and watched how they started to shut in a way that was rather mesmerising. I continued to watch her whilst she lowered her feline head and to my astonishment, she gracefully bowed!

I stood motionless, not knowing quite what to do. Her bow was so majestic that out of pure panic and confusion, I curtsied!

Daisy giggled which irritated me.

She knew I was completely bewildered. That a powerful being had just bowed in front of me, giving me thanks and had no idea why!

Chapter 36

Zaphire's paw touched my hand, which immediately gave me a sense of calm. "Noelle, I know what you are experiencing is overwhelming. Don't be scared, we are so happy to see you."

I just watched her, couldn't really speak or reply as out of nervousness got the hiccups!

"Noelle, calm down, don't be scared. We are your friends and we love you." With those words, Zaphire pranced towards Peter.

She proclaimed to us all in such a captivating way that I was sure the whole universe heard her speak, "You are my children and I appreciate all of your hard work. Our emotions are different to earthlings, our feelings are derived only from our soul."

Chapter 37

Suddenly, she stopped speaking and looked upwards.

In turn we all did the same and heard a sound, a single note, a plain and unassuming tune, which echoed from above. The tune was simple yet magical. It was accompanied by a captivating all seeing light, which made its descent by shrouding Zaphire's soul.

A shadow also appeared and delicately remained at Zaphire's side.

Zaphire stood up on her back legs, gazed at us all and began to speak, "As you all know we have been working very hard in trying to get Ralph's clone better."

She then started to approach all the kids and continued to speak, "His anxiety was making him very ill. Peter observed him all night and am relieved that replacing his negative thoughts with happy thoughts has made him relax and anxiety has ceased. He talked to him in his sleep, giving him tools to use in his everyday life."

She continued to speak in her imperial way, "These tools are happy thoughts and memories, which Ralph's clone will use when he is anxious and sad."

Chapter 38

Ralph added with great excitement, with a smile that seemed to be wider than his face, "My clone is happy now." The kids started to clap uncontrollably. They were so relieved and happy that they had helped with this miraculous cure. The clapping was so infectious that I too clapped in awe of their discovery.

"It was a success!" Peter proclaimed.

The cheering became so loud and uncontrollable that I had to hold onto Daisy's hand. Well, I thought it was Daisy's hand but something was different. I turned to see whose hand I was holding and to my astonishment, it was Tom's!

"Hello, Noelle, I am Tom, your friend's clone." I just stared at him in disbelief. His gold locks, brown eyes, his quirky smile were exactly the same.

However, something was not quite clear. He looked sad or happy, I really was not quite sure. "Tom," I whispered. "Tom, are you OK?"

He then replied, "I have a problem, I have a pain…I have a pain in my stomach, it really hurts." He spoke holding onto his tummy and trying to rub it to make it better.

His deep brown eyes looked into mine. They were full of yearning. "Noelle, I think I am very sick. My stomach hurts so much but Zaphire won't help me."

Chapter 39

I started to panic thinking that my friend, Tom, was in severe pain and was devastated that no one was helping him. Unexpectedly, Zaphire appeared in front of me whilst Peter gently guided Tom's clone to join the others.

"Zaphire, Tom's clone, I mean my friend, Tom, is in pain, in severe pain. Why isn't anyone helping him?"

"Noelle," Zaphire explained. "Noelle, he isn't in pain. He thinks he is in pain. Instead, he is in love and am afraid that is an emotion we can't treat."

I was dumbfounded. "Excuse me, what? Sorry? He can't be in love. He is nine and three-quarters!"

Zaphire started to purr, then gently whispered, "Falling in love can happen at any age."

She then smiled in a see through cat like way and uttered, "Noelle, you are nine and three-quarters. Are you in love?" I went completely red and started to stutter with complete embarrassment,

"Oh, um, well, err, oh, dear." I looked at her with such an awkward smile and uttered, "Maybe?" Then I resumed confidence and denied any knowledge of falling in love but then what sprung to mind was who Tom was in love with.

Chapter 40

I then asked quizzically, "Who is Tom in love with? We tell each other everything!"

Zaphire gently replied, "You haven't told him about us. I presume when Tom is ready, he will tell you." Thoughts went through my mind but had no time to think when Peter arrived smiling in rather a knowing way, which quite honestly I found rather irritating, seeing that he could read my mind.

He then placed his hand in mine and whispered, "I've missed you, Noelle. Come on, let me show you our universe."

He guided me out of the playground and into a field full of flowers. It looked like a vibrant carpet of colour. It was spectacular. "Why didn't you bring me to your world sooner?" Peter just looked at me and replied, "We needed you to grow and grieve."

I then proclaimed, "Did you know about my mum?"

Without any form of emotion, he replied, "Yes, Noelle, we watched."

Chapter 41

I then continued to speak, "I thought none of you were real. I felt you all died with my mum." Tears started to roll down my face. He clenched my hand as he guided me towards a river, that glistened with the reflection of the stars.

"This, Noelle, is the bond that unites us with your world. We manage to get our source of energy from the fish in the lake that give us a magnetic field. It enables us to survive. Do you understand, Noelle?" I was actually perplexed but tried to look as if I understood.

I stared at the lake which looked rather hypnotic. When suddenly he turned my face to look at him, "Listen to me, Noelle, I am giving you information that you must understand!"

He continued, "We help earthlings by giving them parts of their body they require when they are ill, that's why you see some of the kids in our world not complete. We are helping the human race."

Chapter 42

"Do the children from my world know Peter that you are saving them?"

He replied, "No, Noelle, they don't."

He then guided me to see more of the river, which seemed to get larger and stopped. He gazed into my eyes and continued to explain, "We intricately and surgically place an organ in the earthlings or part of an organ that doesn't seem to look as if it is going to survive. Do you understand what I am saying, Noelle?"

"Yes, I do. You must understand this is all too overwhelming!" I then turned my back to him as I didn't want him to read my thoughts and actually felt like crying. The experience was getting to me, after all I was only nine and three-quarters!

Peter approached me whispering,

"Listen, Noelle, we haven't much time and I want you to have the knowledge and understanding of who we are."

I abruptly replied, "I understand what you are saying, you helped Ralph." Then realised what he had just said.

"What do you mean we don't have much time?" He didn't answer, just looked at me in an ever so enchanting way that my heart might have done a flip flop or a three-wheel turn, not sure, just thought he was the most handsome boy I had ever seen.

Chapter 43

"Noelle, you must listen to what I say. It's imperative you retain this information." I just smiled, hoping I wouldn't let myself down by getting hiccups or worse by sweating!

Peter continued to speak whilst looking deeply into my eyes. "We are already twinned or cloned at birth with a human in your dimension. We have the knowledge in helping our twin but our twin has no idea of our presence or existence."

I just watched in awe while he continued to speak,

"Our beings on this star have been born with a gift we are intricate surgeons and have calculated how to save our twins and genetically modify others, who aren't our twins. But that is what I am trying to achieve."

In disbelief, I just stared at him. I then quickly asked, "Do I have a twin?"

Chapter 44

Peter gently moved me closer to the lake. He took my face in his hands, gently caressed my cheeks and leant towards me.

I thought this was it. I was going to have my first kiss with the most beautiful boy in the world or planet or wherever it might be!

My heart started to beat rather quickly. In horror, I started to sweat, which was incredibly awkward!

He moved slightly closer. It was all rather overwhelming as his lips were about to meet mine. When he looked up and saw Zaphire's descent, which was accompanied by music of just a single note.

Suddenly, he stopped and kissed me quickly on my forehead!

After all that he kissed me on my forehead, I thought it was going to be a lovely moment. Irritatingly so, Zaphire interrupted my first kiss!

Zaphire just watched Peter with her penetrating eyes, which gave him the queue to continue what he had to say.

"It's time, Noelle, to show you our helpers from your dimension."

Chapter 45

Peter continued, "I want you to look at the lake, Noelle. You will see the special earthlings that help us." I turned towards the lake and observed a reflection which started to appear. I watched intently and to my astonishment, I saw my father holding a carp fish in his arms. I stared transfixed.

"Peter, that's my dad!" I started to feel quite emotional. "I can't believe it! He always said he worked far, far away!"

Peter gently whispered, "Never be afraid, Noelle, never have fear." I stared bewildered at Peter, then looked at the reflection of my father in the lake.

"Your father has been helping us for years by transporting the fish, by gently placing them in a vortex. It is a lake in your world that brings the fish directly to us."

I stared in astonishment at the lake, then turned to see Peter, who had now transformed to see through whilst Zaphire approached us, together with her faithful shadow by her side.

Chapter 46

She then leapt towards us and started to purr and whispered, gazing into my eyes, "Noelle, are you starting to understand?"

I just nodded while her purring put me into a hypnotic state. I was captivated whilst she continued to speak.

"We are scientists. Some of my children are cloned to children from your planet, however, other clones are being created through our scientific knowledge."

She continued to speak, still continuing to purr, "Your father has been extremely loyal to us. He is a warrior. He has helped us in an immeasurable way. You should be so proud!"

I nodded whilst she purred in an ever so relaxing way that my eyes began to shut. I drifted off into a sleep.

Started to float through the mist.

The stars seemed to be ever so distant whilst I made my descent to my world.

I awoke hugging puppy.

Chapter 47

The next day I tried to phone my dad but he didn't reply.

I so wanted to know whether he helped the other world in sending carp fish to the vortex. In hindsight, it might have sounded rather strange.

I never knew what he did for a living, I only knew he worked far away. I asked Granny what his job entailed but she didn't really know but thought it was something to do with logistics.

Determined to find out a bit more I called Gragra, who started shouting down the phone in pure excitement. The phone must have been upside down as she sounded as if she was in a fishbowl!

Eventually, she realised that she couldn't hear either and started to speak coherently or shout with pure excitement. "Noelle, I can't understand what you are saying but am very busy looking at birdie on my balcony. She's laying her eggs. This time I really hope the squabs survive!"

I interrupted her, "Gragra, I've been having a strange time. I've been having dreams."

Gragra retorted, "Noelle, birdie and I know things, we sense things. You are in love!"

Chapter 48

Saturday arrived. My dad was coming to stay for the weekend.

I was so excited to see him. Unfortunately, he arrived and was extremely tired. I so wanted to talk to him. I was just about to speak when Gragra arrived making her grand entrance and exclaimed,

"I've been talking to two pigeons, not one! Mother sits on her eggs at night and father takes over in the morning. Now will have to repeat all my news to mother pigeon in the evening!"

She made me laugh. I then couldn't hold it in any longer. I blurted out, "Dad, do you help people and help fish?"

He smiled and replied, "I help people, yes."

I continued. "But does it involve big fish like carp fish? Dad, am I making any sense. Is that what you do?"

He looked at me and smiled. "I like helping people and yes, sometimes, I like to go fishing." Granny interrupted the moment by getting dinner on the table whilst Gragra was in huge conversation with my granddad over her pigeons.

Chapter 49

I must admit Granddad seemed rather bored as she had repeated her story various times.

He tried very hard to follow Gragra's conversation whilst getting distracted with puppy running around.

All of a sudden, she loudly proclaimed and announced to us all, "The two eggs have hatched, the most adorable squabs are born."

Granddad jumped out of his seat as her voice was so deafening.

She began to project in rather a shrill way, "I have named them Hope 1 and Hope 2."

Chapter 50

Puppy joined our conversation and placed himself underneath Gragra's chair, hoping to retrieve food that might come his way.

Granny started to talk about my school to my dad, mentioning that we needed to organise a party for my tenth birthday…then all of a sudden she began to cry.

"I miss her, I miss her so much. She would have loved to see Noelle doing well." Granddad quickly got up and hugged Granny.

They both had a moment which was so endearing. My mum was their only child, their pride and joy.

Gragra stopped talking as if in slow motion she turned and stared at me, her stare encompassing and quite mesmerising.

She then proclaimed, "Noelle, sometimes our worlds need to unite. We all have busy lives but what grounds us is the ability to share our pain, love and even stories that have never been told."

With that piece of information, she looked up and gasped. "Look at the moon. Look, it's a full moon. Look, it's so beautiful."

Chapter 51

We obediently gazed at the moon. Granny then uttered, "Noelle, I'm sure wherever your mother is, she is looking at the very same moon."

It was such a special moment, memories of my mother returned in photographic images. Her love of life, her sense of humour and the time we both saw the flying frisbee in the sky.

I started to laugh remembering my mum trying to have a very serious conversation with the chicken pox on the tip of her nose!

Chapter 52

We had a very enjoyable evening. Granny and Granddad decided to recount when they first met and eventually marry.

Recollecting the day of their wedding.

Gragra looked at them in horror whilst she recollected standing with Great Grandfather for a photo and accidentally fell into an open grave!

I couldn't stop laughing. Gragra retorted, "It's not funny, Noelle. My daughter's marriage is tainted by that horrible recollection!"

Granny then got the giggles and retorted, "You even upstaged my wedding!"

"Nonsense child." Gragra replied and continued, "The photographer couldn't find the right light. He kept on asking us to move back. He should have seen what predicament could occur. Thank goodness I didn't break my back!"

It was a fun evening. I went to sleep contented and waited in anticipation for my next journey to the other world.

Chapter 53

I started to sleep and drift slowly upwards into the sky, floated above the moon towards the lonely star that shone so bright.

I arrived in the other world where Peter greeted me with his ever so enchanting smile.

"We don't have much time," he explained. "I need to show you more until we...until we...until we see each other again."

"What do you mean? I don't see you for how long?" I replied whilst tears started to well up in my eyes.

Chapter 54

Peter didn't reply, just took me by my hand and brought me to a laboratory where I saw kids working or watching screens of their twinned clones on earth, meticulously looking at them whilst writing on complicated types of computer software.

Some of the kids had corn seeds and plants on their desks. Peter explained, "We are scientists, synthetic biologists. We are also cloning other children that haven't been cloned at birth. We are recreating, manufacturing clones in order to help the children on earth. We want to eventually help the whole human race but it will take time. We have all become of an age that we need to progress to another dimension to continue our extraordinary work."

He continued to show me the laboratory that was pure white while I saw kids, that were completely transfixed in their work, and Ralph, who seemed to be looking at his plant.

"Hi, Ralph." He looked up at me and smiled. I stared at his plant and said, "What are you doing with the plant?"

Chapter 55

He turned to look at Peter in order to get approval of some kind. Peter nodded, which gave Ralph confirmation to continue to explain. "I am creating medicine through this beautiful flower, a medicine that will help earthlings with any form of disease." I looked at the plant, it was small and bright green. Ralph seemed to adore it. He handled it with extreme care and seemed so transfixed in his work that I continued to peruse the lab.

I was so grateful in meeting such extraordinary kid scientists helping mankind in such an extraordinary way. I saw Daisy analysing her clone on a computer type screen. I excitedly approached her and asked, "Daisy, can you show me what you do?"

With great excitement she showed me her clone, who seemed to have a graph placed on her, divided in rectangles and numbers.

She enlarged her clone on the screen in order for me to have a better look. "You see, Noelle? The graph shows me where we might have to intricately replace a part of my clone if at any time she becomes unwell. We replace either small parts of an organ or the whole organ from this lab." She then continued, "Peter is the one that replaces them as he is the head scientist. He corrects the health of our clones." I looked on in amazement.

Chapter 56

Peter suddenly emerged and joined our conversation. "Noelle, we are biologists. Our mission is to help mankind. We just need a bit of time to create other clones, that is why another lab has been created for us in another dimension." I just continued observing the lab, trying desperately to digest all the information. I really wanted to say that I was only nine and three-quarters and all this information was a bit demanding to retain.

Peter continued, "We need a planet or star that can grow more plants and corn. The seeds are the start of creating human clones and some of the parts are medicine for the human race."

I couldn't believe that seeds or plants could create a human being or Ralph's plant could create medicine. It was so small. I just wanted to say that earth was rather large! However, so many things were surreal on this planet that I continued to listen attentively.

Chapter 57

Daisy interrupted my thoughts and glared at me. "Noelle," she retorted. "You know I can read your thoughts, your world is large but do not ever question Ralph's plant. Please, Noelle, don't underestimate what we do. We work very hard to help all of you earthlings."

I stared in complete embarrassment and apologised whilst trying not to think of anything which was quite hard with all the information I had to retain.

Daisy continued, "We are sad to leave this star but we need more space as things are progressing."

Peter and Daisy both looked at me as if they were expecting me to speak. I quickly thought of something to say but could only say, "Wow!" Which was slightly awkward!

They both stared at me. I realised that finally I had a coherent question to ask. "How do you travel to this other dimension?"

Peter knew I was trying hard to grasp all information and smiled in an endearing way, he replied, "We travel in a shooting star. We sometimes travel to earth to pick up seeds and plants."

Chapter 58

I quickly and excitedly asked, "Does your shooting star look like a frisbee with lights?"

He smiled and continued to say, "Yes, a bit like that, don't you remember, Noelle, we came to see you?"

I couldn't believe what I was hearing and started to speak really quickly as I became overwhelmed and excited. "Yes," I replied. "I saw you with my mum. It was such a special moment." Unfortunately, I started to hiccup as everything was getting me flustered.

Peter smiled and continued, "You see, we are always there. We don't like to go to earth that often as we don't want to be seen too much." My thoughts seemed to speak out loud.

"But don't I see you? I mean don't I see you again?"

"Yes, Noelle," he explained, "but later on when we have grown up a little. You need to live and enjoy your own world. I will always be with you, watching you develop having adventures on earth."

Chapter 59

"I have so many questions," I exclaimed. "I'm not ready to say goodbye."

He smiled and brought me back to the lake and continued to speak, "You wanted to meet your clone. Did you not?" I nodded and quickly turned to see my reflection in the lake.

I just saw myself.

I tried harder to focus but didn't see anything different. I turned to Peter. "I don't see anything. I just see my reflection!"

"Try harder," he retorted. I stood looking in the river but didn't see anything, just a glimmer of myself. The image then started to change; the river began to ripple with the flicker of the moon's reflection.

My reflection's transformation was hard for me to decipher. To my astonishment, my image turned into Peter!

Chapter 60

I got totally confused. "Peter, I don't understand, why have you become my reflection?"

I turned around but couldn't find him but then spotted him leaning against a tree. He started to walk towards me with a grin on his face.

He took me in his arms and gently kissed me on my forehead. He looked deep into my eyes and again grinned. "Don't you understand, Noelle...I am your clone."

Chapter 61

I just stared at him. Frozen with shock. "What? Excuse me, what?"

Peter still grinned. "You heard me, Noelle," he replied.

Still in shock. My thoughts raced, one of the thoughts sprung to mind. *Had I fallen in love with myself?* Peter continued to speak, still grinning.

"We are just different from the other clones."

He took my hand and guided me to a huge type barn and looked at me. He started to try and speak but found it quite difficult, then uttered, "I need to go now."

Chapter 62

I started to stutter, "I will miss you. I will miss our times together." Tears started to fall down my cheeks. "I don't want you to leave me or disappear. You are my friend in my dreams. I'm…I'm alone." I started to cry but Peter gently wiped the tears from my face and whispered,

"No question, my little one, you're stuck with me for at least our lifetimes but we need to grow up a bit."

Daisy appeared suddenly and held my hand as Peter began to leave. He walked backwards, waving goodbye then turned running towards the distant sun proclaiming. "Noelle, remember, we have the world to play with the stars to run away with." He started to fade into the distance, shouting, "I love you, Noelle, can't wait for the day we are reunited."

Chapter 63

"Are you OK, Noelle?" Daisy exclaimed.

I retorted, "No! Of course, I'm not OK. I will miss you all, why do my dreams have to stop, my journeys to you cease?"

She put her arms around me and replied, "For now, Noelle, it's just for now. The elders want you to grow. We will always be here or in a dimension close to here. Zaphire is expecting you. I will take you home once you've finished." I began to get really rather agitated and cross; my temperament began to change.

I was so angry that I stated, "How dare you all do this to me? You have changed my life, my being and now you leave me. I'm so upset so much so that I can't utter any words." With that statement, I again began to my complete frustration. Hiccup uncontrollably. I felt my whole life had fallen apart.

Daisy rubbed my shoulders and whispered, "Calm down, calm down, Noelle. Zaphire will explain. We will always be close to you. Now get a grip. Zaphire needs to see you."

Chapter 64

I walked into an enormous arch like dome shaped area and sitting alone at its centre was Zaphire regal in her pose. In front of her laid a single daisy.

"Welcome, Noelle, to my home." With trepidation, I moved closer, I noticed the daisy had a note attached. I stood transfixed. Zaphire licked her paws. She looked up momentarily and then uttered,

"What are you thinking, Noelle?"

Motionless, I continued to stare at the daisy.

Zaphire continued to self-groom, then stopped.

We didn't speak. She broke the silence by whispering in a rather echoing way, "Do you know what's written in the note?"

"No," I replied.

Zaphire's penetrating look pierced through my soul whilst she continued to speak, "Well, you should know. You wrote it!"

Chapter 65

Without emotion, I answered, "Yes, I wrote a note saying I would love her forever and attached it to a Daisy. I placed it on my mum's coffin." Zaphire moved closer.

"That's correct," she continued to move ever so close to me and uttered, "Remember, Noelle, I am the keeper and protector of souls."

I stared at Zaphire transfixed.

I tried to digest what she was saying but it all seemed extremely surreal.

Suddenly, she excitedly pranced, climbing the walls with delight, athletically running across the ceilings, where I noticed draws and files intricately placed and imbedded throughout.

The shadow seemed to follow her but got caught up with Zaphire's speed and went off in a different direction.

She continued to speak with pride, "These are all my files, Noelle, files on earthlings, clones and my beloved souls. With your help, we will achieve in helping more and more earthlings."

I interrupted her as I wanted to know what I was meant to do, "Zaphire, you mentioned that I am to help in what way?"

She replied, "Your knowledge will help mankind but all in good time…however, for now, it's not goodbye but a pause. You must start living and exploring. Where there is good, there will always is bad. I prevail to keep my souls and my clones protected from not so very good forces."

Chapter 66

I then replied, "Do you mean evil?" Zaphire moved towards me.

"Noelle, when good things happen, there is always a bad energy that wants to emerge. I have given you knowledge, which will enable you to be strong and wise and to never have fear."

I began to cry. I didn't want to leave my other world.

Suddenly her shadow appeared in front of her. It started to get larger and larger, lilac colours appeared beaming throughout the barn, accompanied by a beautiful tune of a single note which echoed throughout.

To my astonishment, a praying mantis appeared. The insect's head started to turn 360 degrees and leapt towards me with a speed faster than light. Her eyes were huge, which got me into a complete state of shock and confusion. Her face came close to mine, gazed into my eyes, then quickly leapt back to Zaphire's side.

Zaphire then spoke in an ever so enchanting way, "Noelle, this is 'Mother'. The head of our universe. She has always been with me whilst observing you at all times."

I had no idea what to say. I was transfixed, getting ever so dizzy when the Praying Mantis's head started to spin again, which made me giggle. "I'm sorry, it's just all so overwhelming." I heard laughter in my head and a voice which echoed.

"Noelle, I don't speak, I use telepathy. Nod if you hear my thoughts." I started to nod profusely. "I'm so glad to finally meet you, please, don't be scared."

Chapter 67

I think I might have gone a pale shade of white as was not sure whether I was imagining the whole telepathic conversation. Zaphire came to my side and whispered,

"You are not imagining anything (Mother speaks telepathically). That's how she communicates."

I began to smile as 'Mother' giggled in my thoughts and mind, projecting me pictures of the universe. The colours were so intense and vibrant.

Stars were multi-coloured, threaded to various moons. I just wanted to jump on them, which made Mother giggle. Some of the dimensions seemed like the sea, a deep blue sea with manifestations of many suns.

Mother's voice began to echo in my mind, "I am proud of you, Noelle, I appreciate you and will never neglect you."

I quickly asked, "But, Mother, are you like magic? Do you look after the universe?" There was a moment of quiet.

She softly responded, "All you need to know is that I will always look after you." With those projected thoughts, she transformed back to a shadow and disappeared.

The music stopped. Complete silence descended. A universal light appeared on Zaphire standing alone, together with the Daisy and note that I wrote to my mother.

Chapter 68

Suddenly, Zaphire leapt and landed very close to my face.

I began to cry out of shock, I suppose.

Everything became daunting but at the same time exhilarating.

"Stop! Noelle. Stop crying. I have something for you…now listen." I tried to stop the crying but unfortunately, I started to hiccup.

Zaphire continued, "I have given you the knowledge of who we are. I will send you a sign that your dreams are in fact a reality. It will appear in your world when you least expect it."

My hiccups stopped. I looked in wonder whilst Zaphire opened one of the drawers from the ceiling.

A pure and transparent ball appeared.

She held the ball of light in her paw, threw the ball up in the air and like magic it appeared by my side.

Chapter 69

I looked in amazement. I really didn't know what to do as the ball of light kept on hopping all over the place. It hopped on her head, it jumped around her as if it wanted to play.

She turned to the ball of light and spoke to it but unfortunately, I couldn't hear what she had said as my hiccups started again. It must have been a command of some sort as the ball of light obediently placed itself by her side.

"Some of my souls get rather excited especially the new ones." Zaphire's conversation seemed to be directed to the ball of light rather than to me as she tried to control its enthusiasm.

Chapter 70

I tried to speak through my hiccups but I couldn't stop as I then started to get the giggles as the ball bounced all over me.

Zaphire watched while she saw me laugh and play with the ball of light. She gave us time to play. She looked onwards and beckoned Daisy to be close by.

"Noelle," she uttered. "It's time for you to go to your world now."

I reproached, "No, Zaphire. I have such fun here. I don't want any of this to end." Zaphire stoically and methodically approached me and in her usual controlled tone whispered,

"This is not the end…this is just the beginning."

I started to feel tired, sleep descended.

My eyes started to shut.

However, I started to giggle as the ball of light placed itself on Zaphire's nose.

It made me laugh while I drifted off to sleep, a deep sleep…a deep, profound sleep.

Chapter 71

I woke up at home with a jolt, hugging puppy and still giggling with the image of the ball of light on Zaphire's nose. I rushed out of bed and decided to call Gragra. I rang and rang and then eventually she answered, "Gragra, I've lost my other world, my dreams. I miss my mum. I miss the other world." With great clarity she replied, "Stop! Stop this nonsense. You have us, your family, even though it might be all not in an order that is perfect. It's time for you to grow up! Do you hear me, Noelle? Nothing in life is perfect. Imperfections is why we learn and how we learn to survive."

She continued with great enthusiasm, "My squabs, whom I've nurtured since they were eggs, have become one. I really don't know what happened to the other one but nature is cruel at times. I am delighted, Noelle, Hope 1 is on his nest and is about to fly."

Chapter 72

I looked out the window. A clear sky full of stars and a moon that shined so bright. I felt contented and protected. Gragra was right. It was time for me to grow up and be thankful and grateful for everything I had. I returned to my room and cuddled puppy and in the corner of my eye, a ball of light swept right passed me. Puppy started to bark, he rushed to the window as the ball of light ascended into the sky.

In all the confusion I noticed a photograph of my mum and I picking daisies on the lawn. It was carefully placed on my bed. Beside it was a fresh daisy, recently picked with a note attached saying,

"I will love you forever."

The End

Book Two
The Black Butterfly

Prelude

She swoops meandering through darkness. Her determination is faultless, her wings glimmer with the reflection of past experiences delivering a melody, surrounded by hope. Dancing in the wind, her destination is nigh, her expectation governed by a single and most simple note. A melody that twins her with her most precious jewel, created by memories of yesteryear. Entranced, she glides above the distant banter, flutters around her most exquisite charm. Caressing her gently, murmuring unassuming tunes of devotion. Revealing self, essence, spirit. She is exposed and murmurs softly a staccato lullaby, don't you remember I am Amaryllis, the black butterfly.

Chapter 1

"I hate you, I hate you…I can't speak, I'm…I'm…I don't know what I feel, Peter, you said you loved me. Why is she here? Who is she?" I raged.

Peter exclaimed, "She is my girlfriend, Geraldine." I just watched in silence. She looked like a mermaid. She had long blonde hair, porcelain skin, she was beautiful. I couldn't utter a word, I was transfixed. She smiled at me in a way that was hypnotic and captivating…she uttered in a whisper that sounded like the rippling waves of the sea.

"I'm so happy to finally meet you, Noelle." I just stared in shock. Anger and jealousy crept into my soul to the fact that my whole body started to shake with rage.

"Excuse ME! You are happy to meet me? Why!" I turned to Peter, tried not to cry but tears of sorrow rolled down my cheeks.

"Peter, you bring me here to the shooting star to introduce me to your girlfriend? WHY!" I started to cry, hiccups arrived as usual, which got me into quite a temper trying to control them through tears of absolute sorrow.

"You have brought me here to the shooting star to show me your girlfriend. Why do I want to do that, why? I thought you couldn't wait for the day we were reunited, that you loved me…but, oh, no! You are with…what is her name? Gertrude? Oh, so sorry, excuse me, is her name Gangrene?"

Peter reproached, "Noelle, stop! Please, stop! Her name is Geraldine. You know that. Just stop!" I turned my back on them both.

"I want to go back to my world now. I want to go home!" Peter became rather red in his face, his multi-coloured eyes became dark, a very deep black. He took my hand, looked deeply into my eyes.

"Don't embarrass me, Noelle, I thought you would be happy for me but I can see you are not. Remember, Noelle, you are just a clone!" I drifted back in a deep, profound sleep, an agitated sleep. I awoke at home hugging Puppy.

Chapter 2

I woke up with a jolt. *Oh my God, it's the first day of school!* I thought to myself. Oh, no exams, tests, many tests…Winter term…The beginning of eternal exams…I just wanted to return back to bed and hug Puppy. Granny started bellowing, "Noelle! Noelle, you must walk through the park today, you will be late for school!" I put my uniform on, ate breakfast and started my journey through the park. I was actually pleased as my lessons were going to be double Science, Maths and English. My favourite subjects, well…actually, my only subjects. I rushed to school, wind going in all directions, a black butterfly or moth got tangled in my hair which I found rather irritating, then it seemed to sit on my face or perch. I started blowing at it to get it off my face but it didn't seem to leave. I burst into tears, remembering what Peter had said that I was just a clone, not his clone, just a clone, maybe I was a clone of no one. I thought I was his clone, I thought he loved me. Tears descended down my face, the butterfly still hanging onto my cheek. My sorrow so deep, my jealousy so intense and of course, she had to look beautiful! And even sound like a mermaid.

"Of course, I had never met a Mermaid but if I had, I am sure she would look like Gangrene or whatever her name was."

Chapter 3

I arrived at the school's entrance and as usual the headmaster greeted everyone by shaking all of our hands before we entered the school. He shook my hand. "Good morning, Noelle, like your butterfly."

I replied, "Good Morning, Mr Bramwell. Excuse me, what butterfly?" He was a big man with a warm endearing face he began to giggle.

"The butterfly stuck to your cheek." I had thought the butterfly had gone a long time ago, obviously it hadn't. I just smiled awkwardly and to my relief it fluttered away.

"Noelle, please meet me in my office. Your grandparents are waiting." Pure dread descended throughout my being, I walked with trepidation and fear towards Mr Bramwell's office. There I saw my grandparents.

I quickly proclaimed, "What's going on? Why are you here? What's happened?"

Chapter 4

Mr Bramwell arrived. "Noelle," he explained. "Your father isn't very well; he is in hospital." I just looked at him in shock, quite honestly, I was more shocked at seeing my grandma put on her lipstick. Mr Bramwell continued, "I know this is rather sudden, I am sure all will be well but I do feel you should be with him." Grandma then started to speak, well she tried to speak but couldn't utter any words. The silence seemed never ending. Mr Bramwell interrupted the dreadful silence and uttered, "Your grandparents are in shock but don't worry, Noelle. I do suggest you leave now to see him." I just stared at him and then looked at my grandparents, who did not utter a word, the silence seemed rather embarrassing that I plucked up the courage and stated,

"Is my dad dead?" Grandma started to cough. It was so embarrassing, it always happened when she got nervous. She tried to speak but gave up while Mr Bramwell gave her a glass of water. Granddad began to proclaim rather loudly,

"Of course, your father is not dead, don't be ridiculous, Noelle. We are just going to the hospital to get the facts of this situation."

Chapter 5

Mr Bramwell calmed everything down by giving my grandma a glass of water whilst uttering, "Noelle, your father has been in an accident in the lake. The doctors think he had an accident fishing. He's sleeping and, in my opinion, you should be close to him." I began to feel anxious, desperation of losing my dad was horrendous. "It will be all right, Noelle, don't be scared but I really do find it important that you are with him." With those words we left. Granny recovered from her nervous cough and smiled, almost curtsied saying goodbye to Mr Bramwell. I just stared in disbelief, was so embarrassed. I really couldn't believe what she was doing. The whole situation was shocking in all different ways.

Chapter 6

Granddad had the car outside the school where Gragra and puppy sat patiently, well…puppy was patient but Gragra was getting slightly irate being left in the car for too long. "I feel in disarray and I am hot and bothered! Didn't know how to open the window!" We got into the car and started a journey that took hours, none of us spoke. We didn't have to, none of us knew what to say. Finally, we arrived at the hospital. We were guided to my dad. I rushed to him and held his hand, he seemed serene in a tranquil sleep. The hospital room was very quiet, too quiet, then with realisation and horror exclaimed, "Where's Gragra?" Panic was written all over Grandma's face.

"Oh, I am in such a confusion, didn't we leave her at home?" Granddad took the map out from his pocket, scanned the map and then very quietly replied, "I am afraid not! We actually left her on the motorway."

Chapter 7

Grandma started to shriek, "On the motorway! When did we leave her on the motorway?"

"When we stopped for petrol," Granddad retorted. Grandma's voice became shrill and hysterical.

"David, you are so so…"

"What are you about to say?"

"Well, I got you here. Didn't I?" Granddad retorted by putting his head in the map,

"Yes, David, you got us here but you left my mother somewhere. This is unforgiveable!"

I then screeched, "Where is puppy! Are you both not understanding! You have lost puppy and Gragra." Grandma then turned to Granddad. "Where is puppy? David, where is Puppy?"

Chapter 8

With despair he proclaimed, "Oh, no! I have just remembered puppy is with Gragra."

Grandma replied in complete despair, "David, why, oh, why didn't you remember we left them behind?" The three of us started to get more and more irate with quite raised voices and completely oblivious to the doctor's entrance. He seemed quite astonished in all of the squabbling and quite honestly, I think we all forgot where we were.

Grandma in a shrill and quite alarming voice stated, "David, why? Oh, why didn't you remember we left them behind?" She became hysterical and started to cry.

"Stop, please!" The doctor proclaimed. We looked at him in disbelief as none of us were aware of his presence. He continued, "You are in a hospital and your relative needs some peace!" We looked at Dad in silence. However, Granddad couldn't remain silent, nor retain his frustration. His face was totally red, he looked as if he was about to explode.

"Judy," he whispered, "you should have realised that your mother wasn't in the car. She usually speaks endlessly about rather useless information!" Grandma stopped crying and in complete despair, retorted in rather a fraught way, "You subconsciously left Gragra behind as you don't like people talking about what you think is useless information, when in fact my mother is extremely smart!"

Chapter 9

Granddad retorted getting redder and redder whilst he tried to suppress his anger. "I did not leave them on purpose, Judy, maybe you should have noticed they weren't in the car." Grandma looked at him in complete desperation and picked up her mobile phone and called the emergency services. The doctor approached to where I was sitting.

"Are you OK?"

I replied with complete exasperation, "What's happened to my dad?"

The doctor replied, "I'm really not quite sure, he was fishing and rather a mysterious fish gave him an electric shock to the fact he has become temporarily paralysed."

I held my father's hand. I clenched it and whispered, "Please, Dad, please." Then ever so gently his fingers started to move and his hand gripped my hand ever so gently. I turned towards the doctor who found himself embroiled in the conversation in trying to find Gragra. I looked at my dad's face, there wasn't any form of expression.

I whispered in his ear, "Dad, what fish has attacked you? What has happened what were you searching for?"

Chapter 10

He opened his eyes and turned towards me. "I was trying to find my soul." With those words he drifted off to sleep. I couldn't believe what had happened to him, how could he have lost his soul? I whispered back to him, clenching his hand and whispered,

"I will do everything to find it." I walked towards the window and looked up in the sky. I so wanted to see my friends from the other world. I so needed their help. I continued to search for the lonely star that existed close to the moon when all of a sudden, the door opened with a huge bang. We all stopped what we were doing. Gragra made her entrance with her eyes nearly popping out of her sockets. She was in a state of confusion and elements of fury were in her expression. She had puppy by her side and surrounded by police.

In exasperation, she proclaimed, "I am furious, how on earth could you have left me on the motorway?"

Chapter 11

Grandma rushed to Gragra's side, apologising and explaining what had happened whilst the police interrogated Grandpa, who was getting flustered and ever so red. The doctor immersed in conversation with the police as well and approached me saying,

"Noelle, what happened? Did your father wake up?" I was holding my father's hand transfixed in watching him breathe. I explained that he had woken up for a bit and uttered a few words and returned to his state of unconsciousness.

Gragra approached me, proclaiming in her rather agitated state, "I really wish all these people would go away. I am so disorientated, anyway, it doesn't matter. I am here for you, Noelle, and I am sure your father will be all right. Have faith. He will recover, remember where there is good there is bad. Look upwards for help. I am sure they will help you." Intensely, I stared into Gragra's eyes.

"Gragra, wait, what? Upwards for help, who will help me? What do you mean?"

She patted me on my shoulders and uttered, "I have to look after your grandparents. Look at them!" I turned to see Grandma and Grandpa still squabbling but silence descended when the doctor proclaimed, "Let's all have a moment of quiet. I would like Noelle to stay with her father for the night as she might be able to get him out of this extraordinary oblivion."

Chapter 12

Everyone left. The silence was comforting whilst I held my
father's hand. Gently, I held his hand whilst tiredness
descended. I placed my head close to my dad's face whilst I
drifted off into a profound, deep sleep. A sleep that beckoned
me into a safe place of deep and profound sleep. I began to
drift up, up into the midnight sky…when all of a sudden I was
brought down, down into the depths of the earth! I was in the
sea! Multi-coloured fish inquisitively observing me. With a
thud, found myself watching a woman doing an exercise
class! Her back was turned so could'nt see her face. She was
a petite woman dressed in black with a very small waist,
dancing to a very strange beat. Her hair was all over the place
due to her extraordinary dance. "Come on, Noelle! Do the
exercise class with me!" I quickly recovered and started to
imitate her dance moves. Thoughts were running through my
mind but didn't have time to think as she shouted above the
beat, "Noelle, concentrate! And to the right, two, three, four
and to the left two, three, four and march. On the spot!" I
thought this was easy whilst looking at the huge window that
she was dancing to. Was trying desperately to see what she
was dancing to, when she shouted over the beat, "Right arm
up, two, three, four. Right arm down two, three, four and

shimmy and shimmy." She shook her whole body to the beat and nearly sat on the floor and with grace, shimmied up to standing position. I really couldn't follow her that by mistake, found myself sitting on the floor. "Keep up, Noelle!" Droplets of sweat appeared on my face and realisation hit me that the exercise class was becoming rather difficult! "Come on, Noelle, and to the right, two, three, four and to the left two, three, four, march on the spot, two, three, four and shimmy, and shimmy! Right fin up, two, three, four, right fin down two, three, four, left fin up, two, three, four and shimmy and shimmy." I was getting rather exhausted though I heard her say 'fin' but thought I was imagining it as sweat was pouring all down my face. The beat continued, "And march on the spot, two, three, four," then she shouted, "Lee, where are you? You are always wondering off. Why aren't you joining the exercise class!" She continued to march to the beat and uttered, "Noelle, carry on with the class. I'm going to find my husband. He seems to always wander off." I thought what a relief. I so wanted to stop the march when all of a sudden I heard from the distance, "And, pirouette, Noelle, pirouette!" I swivelled in rather an uncouth way and found myself on the floor. The woman shouted in the distance, "Come on, Noelle, march two, three, four, march, two, three, four."

Chapter 13

I slowly got up finding the exercise class rather demanding, I looked towards the enormous window she was dancing to and there I realised I was somewhere in the depths of the sea and standing alone was the most incredible being I had ever seen. It was a fish, well, sort of. It looked as if it was a tiny piglet or a tiny elephant. It had four fins. Two seemed like his arms and the other two seemed like feet. He was smiling. I walked up to the window with the beat still playing and placed my hand on the window…the fish like creature mirrored me and placed his fin on the window. I kissed the window. He collided with the window, which made me laugh. Then I heard the woman shout from wherever she was, "Carry on with the class, please." We both ignored her by staring at each other.

I heard in my mind, "Hello, I'm, Joe." I touched the window whilst he did the same with his fin.

"Hello, I'm, Noelle, what are you?"

He telepathically answered, "I'm a fish, a carp fish. I am a Vaquita." I just gazed at Joe. I hadn't seen anything like him before. We stared at each other in silence, smiling. The woman entered the room, her face was beautiful and had bright green eyes. "Good, you have met Joe."

Chapter 14

She continued, "Noelle, you must concentrate whilst I tell you where you are and who we are." She brought me to the other side of the room but I just couldn't stop trying to look at Joe. The woman continued speaking whilst I kept on peeping through her arms at my lovely new friend. I then decided to jump as my excitement got too much. He did the same. "You are not concentrating, Noelle, you must listen." I just really couldn't help myself. With great enthusiasm, I ran to the window and put my hand on my head. He tried to do the same but collapsed laughing as his fin couldn't reach his head. I laughed too and spoke to Joe telepathically,

"Well, at least I didn't get you to do a pirouette!" We laughed and laughed when the woman exclaimed,

"Stop it the both of you! Joe, go and see where Lee is. He is preparing your dinner. I must speak to Noelle and as much as you like each other, I need some calm, please." Joe swam off somewhere around the corner whilst the woman began to speak.

"Noelle, be calm now and listen." I sat down on a swivel type chair, which I couldn't control as it started to spin slowly at first, then rather rapidly. The woman stopped the chair by just giving it a command and calmly began to speak,

"Concentrate, Noelle, please." I gazed in her huge eyes that seemed to get larger and larger whilst she continued to speak,

"We are the elders and live below the ocean. This is a star that we live in."

"Oh," I replied, then quickly retorted, "I'm not sure why I am here. I need to save my father's soul. I thought Zaphire could help or maybe Peter or maybe the Praying Mantis, Mother!"

Chapter 15

"I thought Peter was my clone but he told me he wasn't that, I was just a mere clone!" I began to cry as everything began to get too overwhelming. The woman held my head in her hands and whispered,

"You are his clone, now calm down. All in good time, Noelle." The chair started to swivel slowly at first, turning gently, giving me a sense of comfort whilst music started to follow, a deep, profound, breath-taking tune, which turned into a staccato melody, an enchanting lullaby that drifted me off to sleep. A deep sleep, a sleep that took me throughout the ocean, the deep blue ocean. I started to drift up, up towards the midnight sky. I awoke holding my dad's hand. I continued to watch him sleep and gently said,

"I've met the star in the ocean, I love you Dad." The butterfly descends kisses her loved ones, makes sure they are secure and safe, follows a winding course surrounded by the midnight air, flutters out the window and whispers,

"Don't you understand, I am Amaryllis, the black butterfly."

Chapter 16

Days went by, my dad was still asleep and my dreams didn't bring me back to the other world, which saddened me so. My headmaster was so comforting telling me that everything would be OK, but I was full of anxiety and couldn't really concentrate on my work. I thought that I might be an orphan, alone without parents. The thought was so horrendous that my stomach churned with the thought of losing my dad. I'm sure Mr Bramwell read my thoughts and kept on tapping me on the shoulders whenever he saw me at school to the fact I tried to avoid him so that I wouldn't get that tap which quite honestly became quite annoying! One day he came to my classroom and announced, to my horror, in front of all my classmates, "Noelle, you are going to play a wonderful part in Shakespeare's midsummer night's dream. I have allocated you the part of Puck. The mischievous fairy!" Pure dread ran through my being. I had no inclination nor aspiration in becoming an actress. Therefore, why, oh, why had he done this!!! The classroom went quiet. I went white but Mr Bramwell smiled with delight. I hated speaking on stage, hated any form of presentation as nerves would usually take hold of me to the fact I would become nauseous and hyperventilate. I just smiled at Mr Bramwell and thanked him, not having a clue what my part was and nor what the play was. The whole idea of it all was simply dreadful that I went to sleep that night in rather an anxious state that puppy decided to sleep elsewhere as I kept on twisting and turning. The next day rehearsals began. I was in awe at all the other kids acting so well. I just wanted to be like them. I hoped to be confident like them. Maybe, just maybe I would be like them.

Chapter 17

The day arrived. Opening night of the school play. A midsummer night's dream or let's call it a midsummer nightmare! Grandma and Grandpa arrived with Gragra who projected throughout the auditorium, "My great granddaughter is the lead. I must sit in the front!" She turned to the person next to her and stated, "She is playing Juliette!"

The woman sitting next to her looked confused and quietly uttered, "It's a midsummer night's dream. Your great granddaughter must be playing another part."

Gragra just turned to her in rather a spiky way. "Who are you? Whom is your grandchild? What part does it play?"

The woman said, "I'm one of the leads' Mum." Gragra just smiled triumphant in expectation to the start of the play. Unfortunately, I opened it.

Chapter 18

The kids that didn't have speaking roles were parts of the set. Some were trees, some were different types of flowers, all very colourful. The trees were made of cardboard wrapped around the kids that played the parts of the trees, which incorporated branches attached to their arms. The flowers were colourful types of hats that were placed on the kids that played the flowers, that was ever so encompassing, however, the kids wore them with pride. Then some were fairies with large wings that glittered with fairy dust and their faces painted with silver. We loved our costumes as we worked tirelessly to get them to look perfect. I arrived centre stage, confident and began my speech, "Through the forest have I gone…but Athenian found I none." Whilst I spoke, I had to run through the trees and flowers that were choreographed to move with me but, unfortunately, a tree fell over a flower, who collided into a fairy that toppled over and collapsed onto me. I tried to continue but the fairy got stuck to my costume, dragging the tree across the stage whilst I was desperately continuing to speak. We all got into giggling fits that the other trees and flowers were trying to retain their giggles but unfortunately, they began to shake and eventually they got into such hysterics that the set collapsed. I looked at Gragra, who thought it was wonderful and stood up and shouted bravo! Whilst the rest of the parents together with Grandma and Grandpa and my friend, Tom, hid behind each other's seats with huge embarrassment. We continued to muddle through the play but we really didn't take it very seriously as our giggles took over, as the set was getting very muddled, which made us laugh even more. Gragra thought it was wonderful. She thought it was all part of the show. She couldn't hear so she thought it was the funniest play she had ever seen! I returned home that evening, feeling rather frustrated that it all went wrong. Tom as usual couldn't stop giggling which got me rather agitated as I felt so embarrassed by the performance. However, I then started to collapse in a giggle fit that got Grandma rather frustrated in trying to give us dinner that we couldn't eat. I went to sleep that night, still laughing and hugging puppy.

Chapter 19

I drifted off to sleep, a profound sleep, a sleep that drifted me up towards the midnight sky, then began to descend to the depths of the deep blue ocean. With a jolt, I found myself back on the swivel chair surrounded by the elders. The woman with the bright green eyes greeted me, "Noelle, we have work to do…my name is Luna and the people around me are the rest of the elders that help the star above." They all smiled at me with such beautiful smiles that made me think I should go to the dentist as their teeth were so white. I turned to the big window where Joe was at its centre, surrounded by phosphorescence, which made him glow in rather an enchanting way. "Noelle, I missed you." He was so lovely. I just wanted to hug him. He then whispered telepathically that is,

"You can hug me I can live on land for a bit. I swim through the ocean and lakes." I then turned to Luna who seemed to be in deep conversation with her husband, Lee, and the others with brilliantly white teeth. I just left them chatting whilst I put both of my hands on the window whilst Joe did the same. I looked into his eyes that were blue or maybe brown, black or green. I began to get hypnotised and dazzled by his ever-changing eyes. Luna then interrupted my moment with Joe by proclaiming in rather a demanding way, "Noelle! I need to speak to you. Stop wondering off!" I approached her while she continued to speak.

"You must concentrate and listen to me." I obediently hopped back onto the swivel chair.

"We have been training Joe to do a very important job. He needs to be strong so that he can swim through the ocean and through the vortex to bring the other carp fish to the lake in the star in the sky." I just continued to gaze at Luna whilst she then continued,

"Unfortunately, the star in the sky has been caught up in a time warp and are living in a different dimension through a black hole that has a magnetic power and your father's soul is stuck in this dimension which is in the future. That's why he is asleep because his soul is in another dimension." I just tried to comprehend but found it all a bit complicated.

"Joe is the one that is going to help us and bring the star above to this dimension. Once that has been done your father's soul will return to where it should be." I thought it was all rather complicated.

"But…Luna, does that mean the whole star has disappeared?"

"Yes," she continued. "Yes, the whole star has been pulled through the black hole and the magnetic force that is derived from the carp fish has disappeared. Joe has been training to be strong so that he can swim through the sea and lake to rectify this situation. You will join him through the vortex but that will happen whilst you sleep." I just stared at Luna and the others with white teeth in complete bewilderment whilst the chair started to swivel slowly at first, then quickly spinning me up into the sky then gently bringing me back to my room where I awoke hugging puppy.

Chapter 20

Determination is her flight; her speed is quicker than light or sound her wings begin her transformation reflecting through the droplets of the midnight air echoes of devotion make her flight determined without fear. She is bound by her saviour for her children. She descends to save the echoes of despair, her transformation is nigh, she shouts so that the universe can hear I am Amaryllis, the black butterfly.

Chapter 21

I awoke so glad. It was a Saturday that I rushed out of bed to go and see my friend Tom. I walked through the park; autumn leaves were everywhere that I jumped on them with glee as I heard the crunch which made me smile whilst I began to run through the crisp opaque air. Tom greeted me at the other side of the park smiling. He seemed so happy that I smiled proclaiming, "Tom, I need to tell you about my dreams, my other worlds. I must tell you everything, you are my friend, my best friend!" Then I started to cry. "Tom, it's so overwhelming. I must tell you everything. Have an open mind, please!" He continued to smile.

"Let's walk and talk, tell me all," he spoke so calmly, put his arm around me whilst I told him about the star in the sky and the star below. His eyes were wide open with the stories I told. I felt as if he thought I was hallucinating but he was calm and listened attentively.

"Tom, I need to save my father's soul. Do you understand?"

He gave me a hug and stated ever so calmly, "Noelle, I believe you…" But then began to laugh. "Noelle, you're so funny. You have such an imagination!"

I began to get so upset that I then retorted, "Well, if you don't believe me, well. I have met your clone in the star above, he had a stomach ache and Zaphire couldn't help him as she couldn't treat the earthling clones with a problem that wasn't a disease! She told me you were in love with someone, Tom! That's why your clone thought he was ill." Tom just looked at me, he stopped walking and began to shout,

"It's none of your business, Noelle, none of your business." He then turned and started to run away whilst he proclaimed, "It's private, go away!" I just stared at him running through the fog. I regretted telling him about his clone in the star above but it was the only way he would believe me. I walked home, contemplating the information I had given to Tom and felt ever so sad in hurting him with the information. I knew that he was in love, which in hindsight must have embarrassed him so. That evening, Grandma, Grandpa and Gragra took me to see my dad. The journey to the hospital was so long and Gragra couldn't stop talking about my performance in the play.

"Noelle, you have perfect comedy timing, you really ought to be an actress! The play was so hilarious, I laughed myself to sleep that evening!" I just looked at her and smiled and uttered, "Gragra, the play wasn't supposed to be like that it."

Gragra then interrupted me, "Nonsense, Child, it was brilliant. I've never laughed so much in my life! I think you should become an actress; you were brilliant!"

I then retorted, "No, Gragra, I want to be a scientist. You don't understand. Oh, well, it doesn't matter." I then looked out the window whilst Gragra, Grandma and Grandpa chatted about politics and world events. The journey to my dad was so long. When we got to the hospital, I just ran to my dad, hoping and praying he would be OK. I held his hand, hoping he would clench it but no, it didn't happen.

Whilst I held his hand, Gragra came very close to where I was sitting and whispered, "Noelle, if I were an animal or let's say, if I were a powerful insect, I would be a Praying Mantis and I would be called MOTHER."

Chapter 22

"Excuse me, Gragra? I don't understand, sorry, what did you just say? A Praying Mantis? Called Mother?" Gragra just stared at me, endearing in every way.

"Yes, Noelle, I would be called Mother. Well, I feel that I am the mother to the whole family. Your grandparents need guidance. I feel you have insight so I am not that worried about you…well, you know what to do Noelle. You know how to help your father. I will, however, look after your grandparents!" I just watched her in shock. I thought to myself, *could Gragra be head of the universe? Could Gragra be someone from the other world? Could she really be Mother?* While I looked at her, I started to drift off to sleep holding my father's hand. I drifted to sleep, a deep profound sleep, a sleep that took me up towards the midnight sky towards the full and brilliant moon past the shimmering stars passed the multi-coloured star, then towards a dark hole that took me through a vortex of complete darkness. I felt dizzy with the constant spiral, the spiral that took me into the depths of darkness beyond any forms of time. A time that was beyond the stars, beyond the moons, beyond comprehension, I landed with a sudden jolt on a land that was completely blue. It was completely flat and, in the distance, Zaphire slowly approached with the rest of her children or clones behind her. As usual, Peter was by her side, he was see through so were the rest of the kids. She slowly approached her eyes completely dark in colour. "Noelle, we are in a different world without lakes or sea. We don't have time for survival. We need your help and also your father's help. His soul is in a dimension just below this one. Find him, he needs to help us in order for us to survive."

"Zaphire, I will do what I can, but not sure how. I need to be sent off to sleep." Daisy appeared with Peter through the blue profound mist.

"Noelle," she uttered, "Noelle, we are faltering, we are not surviving." Ralph has begun to stutter again and Peter well, look at him.

"To my despair, Peter's lungs were not so bright, his eyes were dark without soul, my heart sank. He wasn't as beautiful, his soul had disappeared. "Peter," I uttered whilst I slowly approached him.

"Peter, what's happened?" Tears rolled down his face whilst I then began to hiccup to my severe irritation. "You have to help us, Noelle, your father's soul is in a dimension that has been caught in two different time frames. He is king of the sea. You must go and ask his help." Zaphire pranced towards me.

"Your father's soul lives close to the sea, a sea that is silver and white, a sea that you have never seen before. You need his soul to help us or let me say it in another way, his clone needs to help us." My hiccups stopped.

"Wait, what? I don't really understand, does my dad know his clone is the king of the sea? Sorry, I mean the silver sea? Oh, I'm so confused…I really am and feel so desperately sad that you are not shining so bright." Zaphire approached very closely, her feline face practically touched my nose and began to purr, a hypnotic purr that lulled me into a sleep, a deep profound sleep, a sleep that brought me upwards through the dark hole to a dimension within the darkness to a beach of sand of silver that glittered whilst the white and silver waves played with the reflection of the sparkling sand. It was breath-taking, absolutely breath-taking. I then noticed in the middle of the sea a figure was sitting on a chair with gigantic fishing rods by his side. He was looking out to sea; however, I couldn't see his face as the mist made it hard for me to decipher who he was. I watched him look out to sea. I then proclaimed, "Dad! Dad, is that you? Dad?" His body seemed to freeze, then immediately turned towards me. His face gleamed with complete happiness.

"Noelle, my beautiful Noelle," he shouted over the noise of the waves. "Noelle, I'm so happy to see you." He then dived into the silver ocean through the waves and arrived on the brilliantly white sand. We both starred at each other smiling with complete delight. I ran towards him and hugged him crying, "You are awake, Dad, you are awake, Dad. I am so happy, I'm so utterly happy." He hugged me and shouted through the wind that echoed throughout the universe, "Amaryllis, Amaryllis."

Chapter 23

She sweeps as she hears her name, her velvet wings clip the frosty air. Her descent determined with her flight, hearing voices of delight echo throughout her transformation in the midnight air. Her king awaits, a surprise awaits. She hears her name, her transformation begins whilst diving into an ocean of silver and white. With delight, she proclaims with complete devotion, "Yes, it's me, I'm here. I am Amaryllis. Yes, it's me. I'm Amaryllis, the black butterfly!"

Chapter 24

Dad and I laughed and played. There was something different in his appearance, it was if he was taller, stronger and had a hat that was attached firmly to his head, a hat that wasn't really a hat, it was like elastic stuck to his head. He seemed like a warrior. He seemed different but I didn't care whatever his appearance, I didn't care. I was so happy being with him when all of a sudden, he turned towards the sea and within the midst, a woman with blonde hair draping her body. She had wings, black wings which, in slow motion, wrapped around her petite frame. She slowly walked towards the shore, where I saw she had a tail like a mermaid. "Oh, my, God, it's you, it's you, Gangrene, sorry, oh, so sorry, Gertrude, oh, dear." I desperately tried to search my brain to remember the name of Peter's girlfriend.

"Noelle, you know who I am. I am Geraldine. We met on the lonely star next to the moon."

"Yes, of course, Geraldine." Her tail seemed to be able to walk but she wasn't really walking as a foot of transparent or air was underneath her. She didn't touch the ground. I was completely hypnotised by her beauty. She held my father's hand and approached me, holding out her hand, tears were in her beautiful green eyes quite honestly was rather confused how could she be holding my father's hand when she was Peter's girlfriend! They both came up quite close when she started to transform. Her blonde hair became dark brown and her eyes shone with the glitter of the white sand. She began to smile. I was mesmerised, her transformation was enchanting. She uttered, "Noelle, do you recognise me?" I stared at her. I couldn't utter a word. I just stared transfixed.

In overwhelming shock, I desperately tried to speak, "Yes, I…um…I know who you are." Tears began to fall down my face. The mermaid approached ever so close. I then whispered, "You are 'mm'." I couldn't say her name as joy, pure joy enveloped my whole soul. "You are Mummy, my mum! You are my mother." She then held me whilst saying, "Yes, Noelle, I'm Mummy. Yes, my dearest Noelle, it's me, Amaryllis, the black butterfly."

Chapter 25

My mum just hugged me with my dad embracing us both. I began to feel ever so tired. I drifted off to sleep, a deep profound sleep, drifted through the silver and white air. Moved higher and higher into the dark sky, spinning through a dark hole that guided me twinned with a very shrill sound that powerfully moved me up, up into a sky of stars surrounded by the moon, where I started to drift downwards, gently drifted through the clouds, through the atmosphere. I awoke in my bed hugging puppy.

Chapter 26

The next day was a rush to get to school. Grandma decided to drive me to school which was rather a mistake as she got flustered with a never-ending roundabout. It was never ending as we went round and round as she couldn't find the exit.

I started to drift to sleep as got so dizzy in her driving, round and round a roundabout.

My eyes started to shut by the never ending turning that I drifted up, up into the clear blue silver sky, past the moon, past the glittering stars, then floated down embedded in a cloud that gently placed me in the dark blue sea landing in a swivel chair that went round and round. My eyes opened.

"Noelle, we have work to do!"

I just stared at Luna's ever-changing eyes and to my delight, I saw Joe. He was glowing, I ran to touch the glass screen where I put my hand on it. He echoed that with his fin.

"Noelle, we have work to do and we don't have much time. We have to save the star above." Luna was rather too direct or authoritative, which made me hiccup, which got me rather frustrated.

Luna's husband, Lee, arrived. "Noelle, you do realise we are training Joe to do something rather special. He has to swim through the sea, through the lake, where he will arrive in a vortex that twins the star to your world. He needs to do this so that the carp fish can give the life to the star in the sky." I just watched him and then looked at Joe and thought this wonderful fish is going to save the star in the sky and save my father's soul. Lee continued to speak whilst then getting distracted by the elders with brilliant white teeth that congregated towards the window. They just all looked at Joe. A deathly silence descended, which made me feel rather scared. One of the elders with white teeth commanded,

"Joe, it's time now. Do what you have to do. We will meet you again. Once you have done what you are set out to do." I then saw terror in Joe's eyes.

I then proclaimed, "If he can be on land, let me hug him. He's my friend. Please, don't let him leave, I love him." Luna and Lee started dragging me away whilst I began to sob uncontrollably. "It's dangerous! You know it's dangerous," I continued to sob. Joe approached the window and reached out with his fin and telepathically said,

"I love you, Noelle, I will be OK." I then retorted so that they could all hear me. "I want you to never leave me. I want to give you a hug. For I want you to know that you will always be with me. I love you, Joe!"

Luna then spoke to the elders whilst I sobbed uncontrollably, knowing full well that my special friend might never return. "Noelle, we will bring Joe to you in a compartment of our home, follow me." I did so. I followed her to a compartment where Joe was waiting. I ran to him. "Joe, please, Joe…please, be strong. I love you; I really do. You are saving the star in the sky. You are also saving my father's soul." His fin touched my head, his bright clear eyes stared into mine and spoke,

"I am prepared for my journey; I know what to do. I will deal with what I have to do but you must promise me something."

Still sobbing I retorted or mumbled, "Yes, anything, Joe, anything."

"Be strong, remember, you are cherished. You have insight and the knowledge." I put my arms around Joe, still crying whilst Luna and Lee dragged me away from him and put me back on the swivel chair. The swivel chair started to turn slowly at first, then quickly throwing me out of the ocean to the brilliant blue sky where clouds gathered to gently place me back in my grandma's car going round and round the roundabout…

"Finally!" she proclaimed. "Finally, I have found the exit! You will only be two minutes late for school." I felt dazed, distraught and anxious. I really didn't want to go to school; too many emotions encompass my soul. The idea of Math and further Math and whatever else was happening at school that day just filled me with dread. I wouldn't be able to concentrate. How could I tell anyone about my experience, my deep profound experience? How could I say I loved a fish? A fish that spoke, they would think I wasn't living in reality, but I had conquered something I had conquered insight. I had finally conquered a reality of insight. I felt it was a gift a true gift. I had the knowledge of something remarkable and inexplicable.

Finally, we got to school where Mr Bramwell was shaking all the pupil's hands. Grandma and I approached Mr Bramwell. "Noelle, good morning and good morning to you, Judy." His warm smile again got Grandma in a coughing fit whilst she spluttered,

"I'm sorry we are late. I just got desperately confused with the roundabout." I just felt so embarrassed as she seemed to get rather nervous whenever she saw Mr Bramwell.

The day seemed to drag. I just kept on looking out of the window, thinking about my journeys to the other world, a world that is divided in two, through a dark hole that takes you to the future, a world that is trapped. I was just so happy, so extremely happy to have met my mother, my beautiful mother, Amaryllis, the mermaid, the black butterfly.

Chapter 27

Days went by, I wasn't taken anywhere through my sleep, which saddened me so. I walked with Grandma and Granddad through many beautiful walks with puppy in the countryside. My granddad turned to me on one of my walks. "Noelle, dig deep, dig deep into the memories of the past."

I just looked at him and uttered, "What do you mean, Grandpa?"

He held my hand and uttered, "Dig deep into the memories of the past, you will find so many answers to your never-ending questions that reside in your mind." I really had no idea what he meant as his words were so profound. I loved my grandparents so much. I really wanted them to know I had met their daughter in the other world. I really wanted to tell them everything but it wasn't the time. That evening I called Gragra. I so wanted to know why she would call herself mother, why she would be a praying mantis if she were an insect, I so wanted to understand. "Gragra, you told me that if you were an insect, you would be a praying mantis." As usual she couldn't hear.

"A dentist?" she retorted. "I'm certainly not going to the dentist."

"No, Gragra, please, repeat, you said that if you were an insect, you would be a Praying Mantis called Mother." She then shouted as obviously she couldn't hear,

"What are you saying, my dear child? I'm not going to the dentist and if your grandmother is taking me to the dentist, I'm not going." The conversation was brief as she couldn't hear which made me so frustrated. I needed to talk to her but it seemed such an issue. I just gave up. That night, as usual, I fell asleep hugging puppy.

Chapter 28

The day dragged on and on, I couldn't wait for the bell that rang to finish the day...I ran home through the park, ran and ran through the autumn leaves, ran with my heavy books in my bag but its weight didn't bother me. I ran through the crisp air. I ran to get home. Out of breath I approached home, ran through the door and there standing in the middle of the sitting room was Gragra holding a cup of tea. "Hello, Noelle." Her back was turned whilst she sipped her cup of tea. "How have you been?" I just watched transfixed as I couldn't utter a word. "I've been...Um, well...I have had journeys, Gragra...um, then I started to hiccup which was most unfortunate."

"Stop, Noelle, stop. Don't be nervous. I'm Gragra. I love you and admire you." Her back was still turned and I couldn't see her face. I stood motionless thankfully my hiccups had stopped.

"You do realise I know about your journeys to the other side of the moon and your journeys to the deep blue ocean." I stood transfixed watching her with a controlled and ever so feline way sip her tea. "Gragra, did you know? Do you know what's happening to me?" Without turning she uttered,

"Yes, my dear, Noelle, after all I am MOTHER!" I just watched transfixed. I couldn't believe what she had just said I just watched her sipping her cup of tea. In silence we were. I just had to digest what had just been said. I had to digest the fact that my great grandmother was the head of the universe. Her body then began to change, her legs became insect like, her head then turned 360 degrees. She lunged quicker than sight or sound. It appeared right in front of me.

"You must listen to me carefully, Grandma and Grandpa don't know who I am but your mother has always known. You have been chosen, Noelle. You have been chosen before you were born. You will take my place one day." I just stared at her transfixed seeing my Gragra's head turn 360 degrees was rather mesmerising. We just looked at each other. In silence we just stared, her eyes transformed in such a big way. Then all of a sudden, I heard a crash in the kitchen.

"Oh, no," Grandma squeaked. "My cake, it's just fallen onto the floor."

Chapter 29

Days went by and I visited my dad regularly seeing him sleep. I saw Tom, my friend, Tom, and we walked together in the park with puppy. We knew something and walked in silence as we both felt so at ease in both our company that we didn't have to speak. Well, I really wanted to know more about who he was in love with but it didn't matter. I just thought that I was lucky to have such an incredible friend. A friend that would look out for me, a friend that is who would take care of a friend that I would have forever. That I would love forever.

Chapter 30

I went home that evening and had tea with Grandma and Grandpa. We chatted about my schoolwork, then all of a sudden, I blurted it out, "I have seen Mum…Mummy in my dreams, my other world."

Grandpa then whispered, "Amaryllis is always in our thoughts and dreams…" Grandma then hugged Grandpa and turned to me.

"Amaryllis is also within you. Her soul must be beside you, guiding you." I rushed towards them and the three of us hugged each other. Tears rolling down our cheeks, remembering Mum, my beautiful mum. It was a moment that I would and will always cherish forever. She swoops with determination, her flight is measured with anticipation, her wings clip the snowflakes in the air, her black wings begin to shimmer reflecting moments of yesteryear. Her descent is graceful caressing her young while they sleep murmuring such gentle melodies, staccato in tone she whispers, "Don't you remember, I am Amaryllis, the black butterfly."

Chapter 31

I hugged puppy hearing voices in my sleep, I just hugged my puppy for comfort, scared and bewildered. I tried to shut my eyes so that I could help Joe or do something to bring my father's soul back. I just wanted to do something but really had no idea what. I just thought that maybe I would just have to be patient, just wait a little while for my sleep to take me to the star above or the star below or the other star that was caught up in time through the black hole through the vortex, where my father's soul resided with his mermaid, my mother, Amaryllis, the black butterfly.

Drama exam woke me up with all the words in my head as Gragra thought I should be an actress after seeing me in mid summers night dream or nightmare as it was, however, she thought it was the most hilarious play she had ever seen. Of course, it was funny as the set had completely collapsed! Anxiety took over my whole being when I walked to school and shook Mr Bramwell's hand. "Good luck for today. You will be brilliant; you will pass your drama exam with flying colours!" I really didn't think so. I thought they were all trying so hard to give me confidence as I was always shy and perhaps rather awkward. I watched the clock on the classroom wall tick to 11.30. I really wasn't listening in my French lesson, I just wanted not to hear the teacher as I was petrified, I would do my acting speech in French!

After the lesson I approached the room where my acting exam was to take place. I opened the door and to my relief no one was there. Mr Bramwell appeared all in a fluster. "Noelle, I am so sorry but the examiners car has broken down. She will be slightly late. Just rehearse until she gets here." I was so relieved I started to repeat my lines in my head but I drew a blank. I couldn't remember anything. Terror shook through me, anxiety made me tremor. I just so wished the examiners car would never start again that she would be stuck and that I wouldn't have to recite such complicated verse.

The door opened. I looked at the examiner. I watched her whilst she slowly approached. She sat down with her notes and with a wonderful smile gazed into my eyes. "Noelle, please state the piece you are about to do and let's begin." I froze in shock as her feline features began to change. It was as if in slow motion she metamorphosed into Zaphire!

"Zaphire? Zaphire? Is this really you?"

"Yes, it's me, Noelle. It's me." Her whole body changed and before me stood the queen of the star above her features as beautiful and bewildering as before, she began to purr and stated,

"Noelle, use your knowledge. I am always here for you but you must guide Joe to a place we will all reunite. Your father's soul has to take him out of the water and when that happens the stars return to their natural place."

I then uttered, "Mm, well, just a little question, do I have to recite my poem to you?"

"Don't be ridiculous, Noelle, you have already passed in my perception but the examiner is still in the car! She will have to determine whether you have passed or not. Whatever happens, whether you pass or fail, it really doesn't matter in the whole spectrum of life. It really doesn't matter." She then began to purr which sedated me so that when the real examiner arrived. I will be calm and wasn't bothered even if a few of my verses were in French! At that stage, I didn't really mind of the outcome, even though the verse might have sounded rather odd but my main aim was to get home and drift off to sleep.

Chapter 32

I held my puppy, my gorgeous puppy, even though he wasn't a puppy anymore but that was OK. He was an adult, a sturdy adult that exuded so much love and affection. I held him there for and drifted off to sleep, a deep profound sleep, a sleep that took me up towards the moon, drifted passed to a dark hole that brought me down to a place that was unknown, a place that had a garden with empty chairs. There were two chairs at its centre and chairs that situated beside them. There was a climbing frame at its centre and wooden type steps beside it.

I felt alone, not really knowing what to do. I just sat on the floor and waited for something. Actually I had no idea what. In front of me was water, clear blue shimmering water which made me so happy just by watching the rippling of the water. Whilst I watched, the ripples started to separate and out of the water, my dad appeared in a soul like form holding onto his mermaid. They swam towards me accompanied by a gentle melody that echoed throughout the ocean. "Noelle, this is an important moment, join us." They both sat down on the two chairs, holding hands and looking at each other with so much love in their eyes. I turned around as out of the water the elders appeared followed by Luna and Lee. They all seemed to sit beside my most beautiful parents. The water started to move, it was as if something was appearing or coming forward from its centre. Behold, Zaphire arrived with Peter, Daisy, Ralph and all the clones. I just watched them all taking their seats beside my mum and dad. I looked at Peter who seemed not so beautiful, not so enchanting as before, Daisy looked tired and Ralph seemed to continuously stutter.

Then silence, a deep apprehensive silence. It seemed to be an everlasting silence, a silence that was so cold that I started to shiver. I knew we were expecting Joe, my beautiful Joe. The anticipation was endless, then with a sense of calm the waters opened. Joe's beautiful face appeared through the shimmering water. Tears of delight enveloped my soul. My father approached the water's edge and stroked his head and brought him up to stand in front of all of the elders, in front of Zaphire and Peter and the clones. They all bowed in complete respect to Joe. I fell to the ground and kneeled, opened my arms to Joe. "You did it, you did it! I love you so very much. You actually did it! You did it, Joe!" His fin reached out to me and I held him so tight.

"Well done, Joe," I whispered.

He replied, "I am so honoured to have met you, Noelle."

"What do you mean, Joe? You are the next in line to the universe. Don't you understand?" I turned towards my parents when all of a sudden the water became turbulent, waves going in every which way when suddenly the praying mantis appeared separating the waters, her wings lilac with colour that turned the waters to her reflection. It was my Gragra, my great grandmother. She was accompanied by an assuming note followed by a simple melody that echoed throughout the universe. My mum went towards her, where the praying mantis enveloped her with pure love, then beckoned me to

147

join the embrace. My mother then returned to my father whilst the praying mantis turned me to face the elders. Zaphire and Peter approached me and bowed to my complete bewilderment. Peter became beautiful again, Zaphire, Daisy and Ralph where by his side, Zaphire started circling around me, her beauty became spell bounding. She uttered "Peter has something to say".

Peter took my hand and showed me the water. I noticed Daisy and Ralph looked happy again I felt a tranquillity that gave me a sense of calm, again. Zaphire announced to all whilst majestically opened the waters of the sea and exclaimed "Noelle look into the water." Peter uttered "Noelle look into the water, see your reflection." I looked into the water and saw a beautiful black child looking straight at me, her satin skin was beautiful she was smiling and so was I. I turned to Peter, "I don't understand." He brought me further to the ocean, "look closely Noelle," I kept on looking at this beautiful black girl but couldn't find myself in the reflection.

"I see a beautiful child but I can't find my reflection." Peter clenched my hand and whispered, "that is your reflection, you forgot what colour you were when your mother died, you forgot who you were". I looked at the water in complete shock I stared at my beautiful black satin skin I was so shocked, couldn't believe that the beautiful girl in my reflection was me. I became strong, complete. With tears in my eyes I felt a sense of relief to know, finally my identity. In a spell bounding musical harmony guided by the ripple of the waves of the deep blue ocean.

The praying mantis shouted so that all the universe could hear. "This is Noelle, Noelle is her name. She has the knowledge. She has brought us all together again. Noelle," she proclaimed, "Noelle, you are now and from now on known as 'The Black Butterfly'."

Chapter 33

She swoops, caresses her beloved jewel and bids farewell for one moment. Her insight can foretell their embrace will remain endless. Drawn to the midnight sun, she descends and places her father's soul upon her wings, entwining with the midnight air, she bows with respect to her most enchanting friends, says a goodbye to her mother whispers melodies of love, heroically flies through winds and storms places her father to human kind embraces her love of three different worlds shouts in a melody that is so clear, yes it's me, yes I am, do not fear, yes I am Noelle yes it's me, I am the black butterfly.

The End